USBORNE FIRST READING
Level

10635742

How the
Leopard
got his Spots

by Rudyard Kipling

Retold by Rosie Dickins

Illustrated by John Joven

Reading consultant: Alison Kelly

Once, the leopard
had no spots at all.

This story tells how
things changed.

Long ago, everyone
lived on the light,
sandy plain.

Everyone had
light, sandy skin.

Then, Zebra and Giraffe found a forest.

What's in there?

Let's find out!

In the dark, they
grew dark patches.

They hid in
the shadows.

The man hunted.

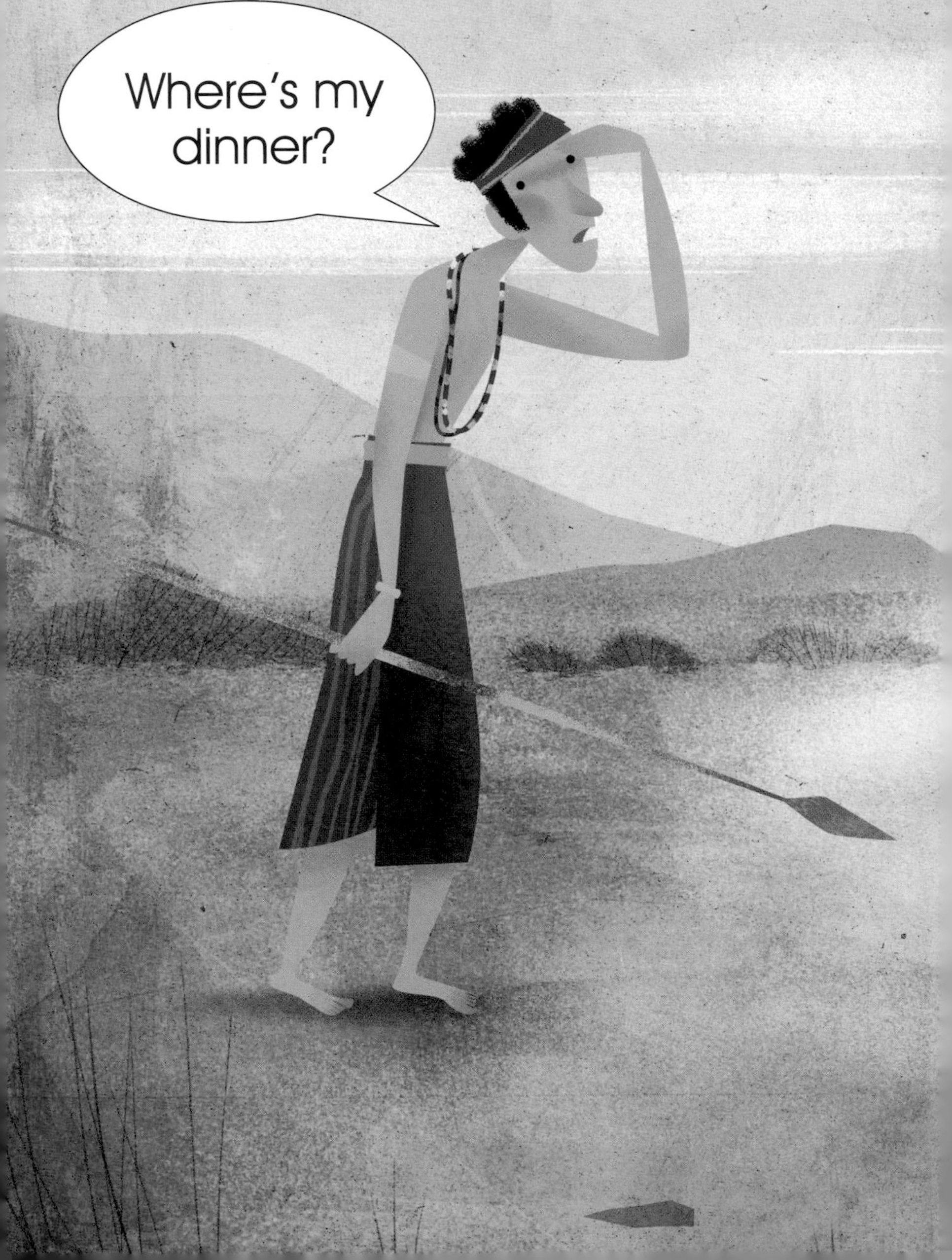

Leopard hunted.

They hunted
in the forest.

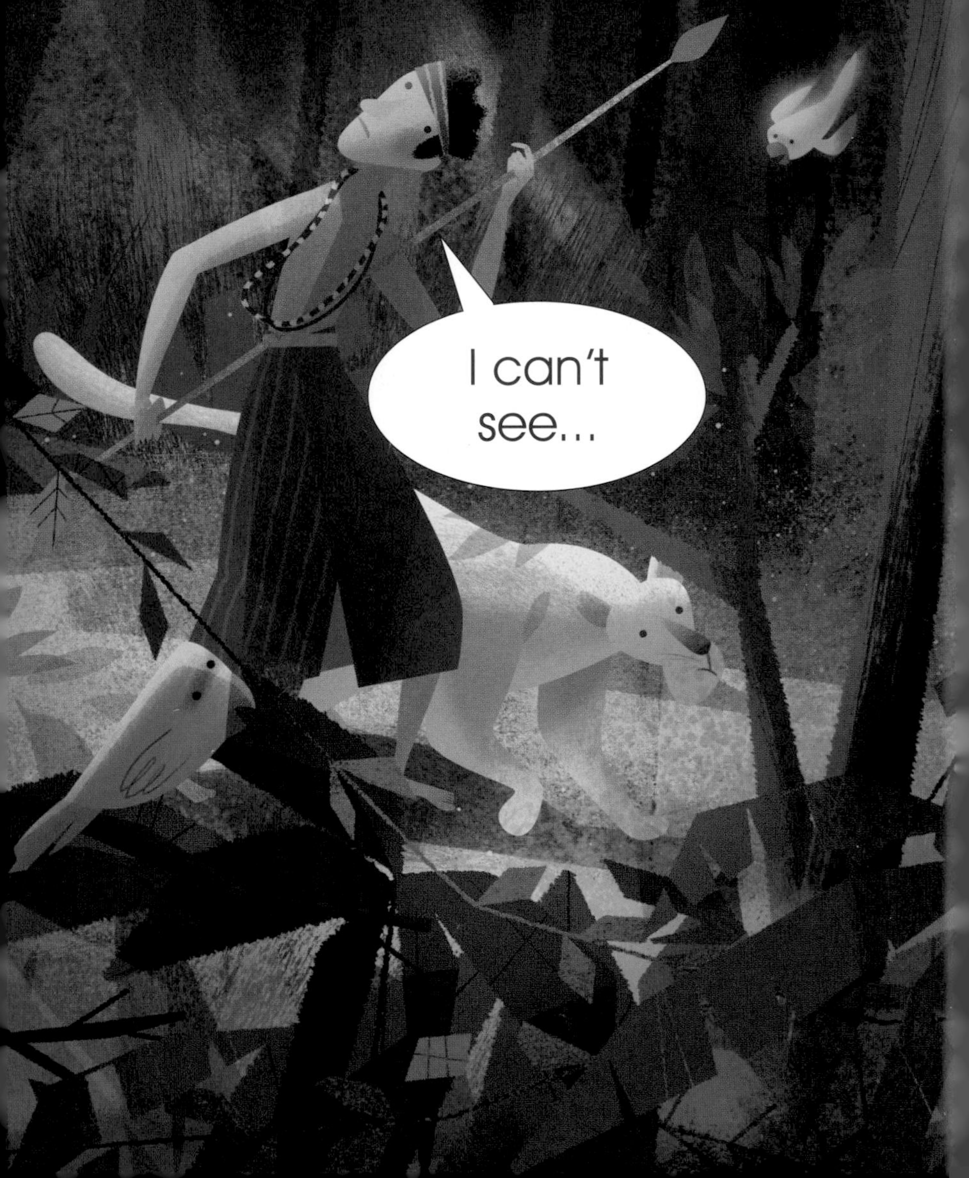

At last...

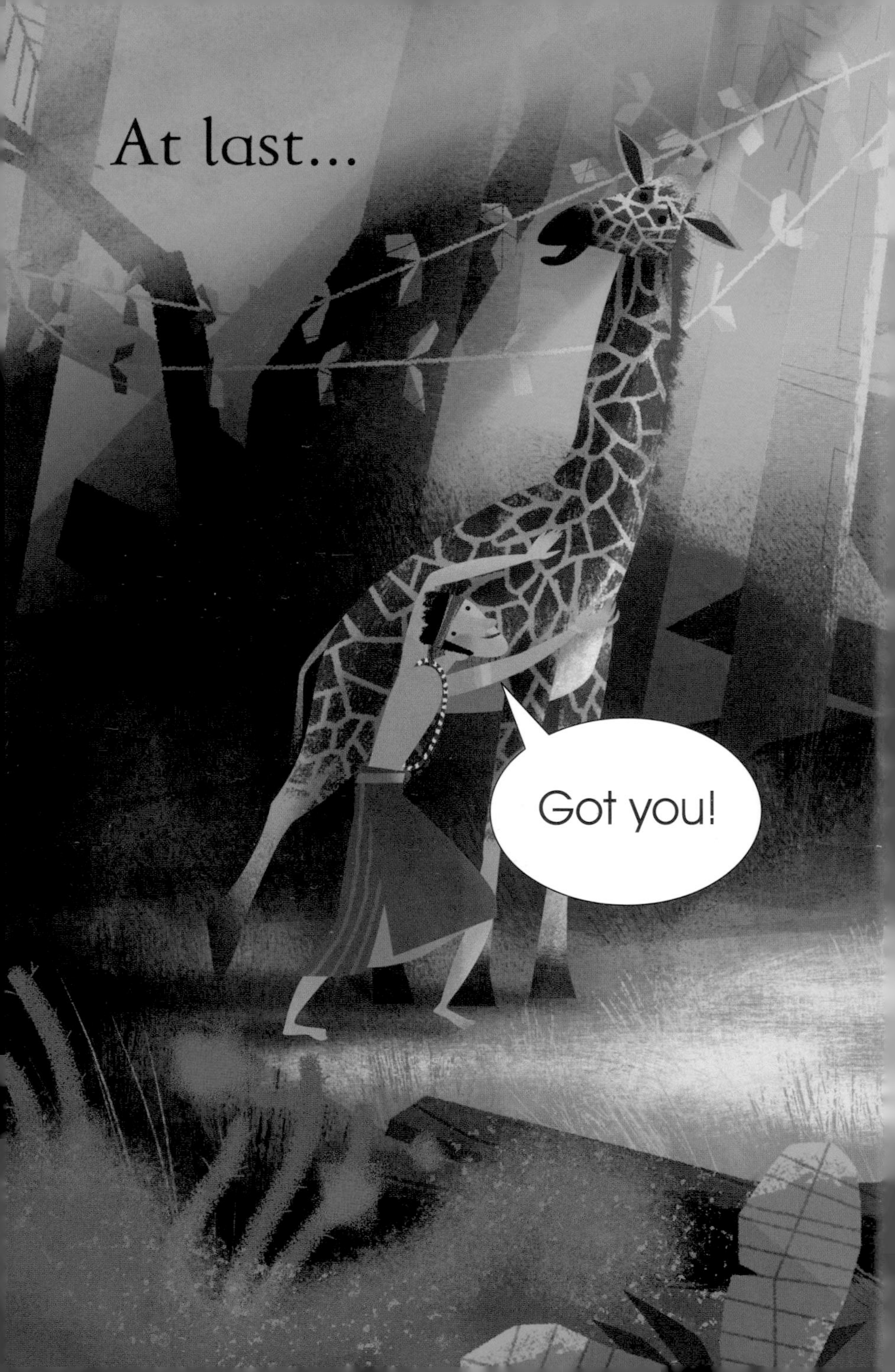

Then the hunters let go.
They were puzzled.

"Why have you
grown patches?"

Zebra and Giraffe took
one, two, three steps...

Zebra and Giraffe
were gone!

“I can do that,”
said the man.

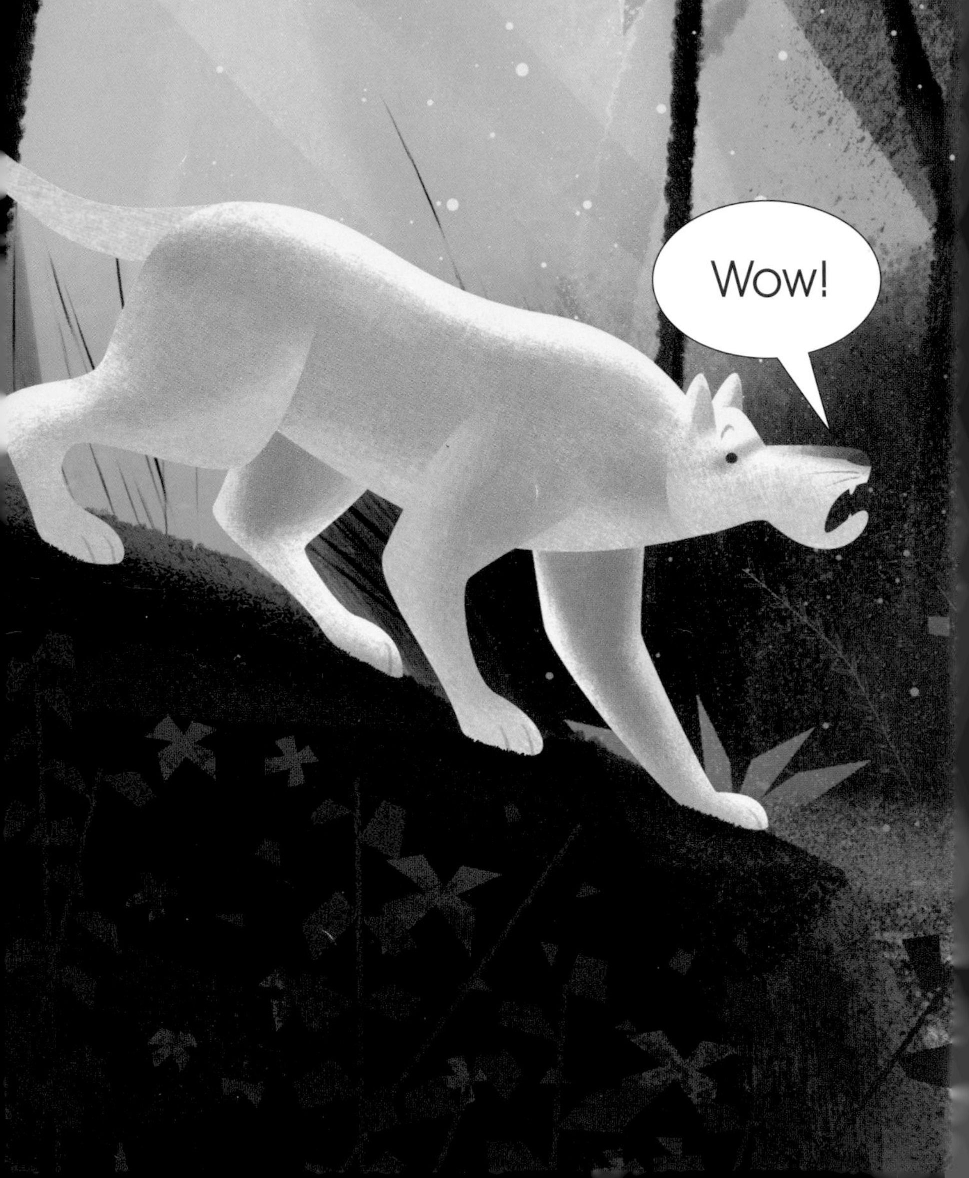

He wrapped
himself in shadows.

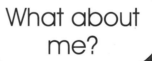

The man held out
a hand.

He made shadowy
fingerprints.

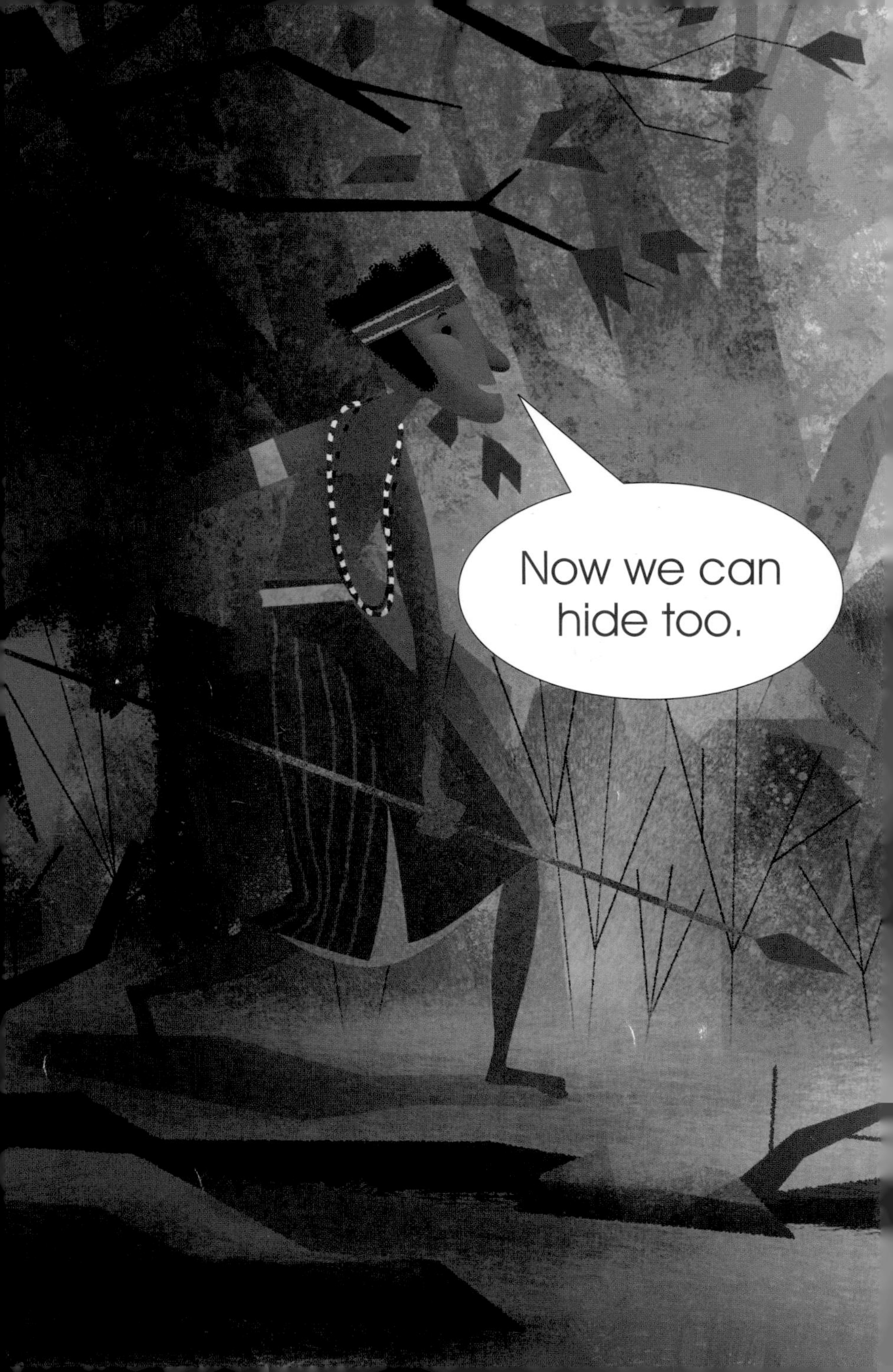
Now we can hide too.

So that's how the
leopard got his spots.

PUZZLES

Puzzle 1

Finish the sentence.

Once, the leopard
had .....

pink spots.

flower pots.

no spots at all.

Puzzle 2

Put the pictures in order.

A

He made shadowy fingerprints.

B

"Now we can hide too."

C

He covered himself in shadows.

Puzzle 3
True or False?

The man
caught
a cold.

The man
caught
Giraffe.

Leopard
caught
a fish.

Puzzle 4

Spot five differences
between the two pictures.

Answers to puzzles

Puzzle 1

Once, the leopard had no spots at all.

Puzzle 2

C He covered himself in shadows.

A He made shadowy fingerprints.

B "Now we can hide too."

Puzzle 3

The man
caught a cold.
<u>False</u>

The man
caught Giraffe.
<u>True</u>

Leopard
caught a fish.
<u>False</u>

Puzzle 4

About the story

This story is from the book *Just So Stories* by Rudyard Kipling, which tells how animals came to be the way they are.

Designed by Sam Whibley
and Laura Nelson
Series designer: Russell Punter
Series editor: Lesley Sims

First published in 2017 by Usborne Publishing Ltd., Usborne House, 83-85 Saffron Hill, London EC1N 8RT, England. www.usborne.com
Copyright © 2017 Usborne Publishing Ltd.

USBORNE FIRST READING
Level Two

Usborne First Reading
The Magic Melon
Retold by Rosie Dickins
Illustrated by Sara Rojo

Usborne First Reading
Little Miss Muffet
Retold by Russell Punter
Illustrated by Lorena Alvarez

Usborne First Reading
How Bear Lost his Tail
Retold by Lucy Bowman
Illustrated by Ciaran Duffy

Usborne First Reading
Doctor Foster went to Gloucester
Retold by Russell Punter
Illustrated by David Semple

Usborne First Reading
There Was A Crooked Man
Retold by Russell Punter
Illustrated by David Semple

Usborne First Reading
Clever Rabbit and the Lion
Retold by Susanna Davidson
Illustrated by Daniel Howarth

Usborne First Reading
The Dragon and the Phoenix
Retold by Lesley Sims
Illustrated by Graham Philpot

Usborne First Reading
Stone Soup
Retold by Lesley Sims
Illustrated by Georgien Overwater

Usborne First Reading
King Donkey Ears
Retold by Lesley Sims
Illustrated by Mike and Carl Gordon